DIARY
OF A
MINECRAFT
KITTEN

BOOKS KID

TABLE OF CONTENTS

Day 1

I am Slinklebert Petrovius Mordechai Smythe, but everyone calls me Slinky, mainly because nobody can ever figure out how to say my name properly.

I live in the jungle with my family and we're the royal family here. It's no big deal really. It just means that every now and then, dad puts on a crown and makes people bow to him, just so they know who's boss. And once a year, we have a special party for all the important Minecraftians in the area so dad can show off how many emeralds we have.

It's very boring if you ask me. Nobody ever does though. I'm just a kitten and nobody thinks that I have anything to say they want to listen to.

That's OK with me. I don't want to be royal anyway. I'd rather play all day. That's why I'm glad we live in the jungle. There's so much cool stuff to do here. I can climb trees, chase sunlight through the leaves, and catch fish in the lake. It's a busy life being a royal kitten.

It's going to be my birthday soon and dad asked me what I wanted. I told him that I wanted to have a pet creeper.

He told me not to be so silly. Everyone knows that creepers don't exist. They're a story made up by Minecraftians to scare naughty children. No ocelot has ever seen a creeper, and if nobody has seen one then they can't be real.

It's a shame they're not real though. They sound so cool! I mean, tall, green things that blow up when they're annoyed or frightened or trying to cause trouble? Who wouldn't want to meet one of those?

Since dad said I couldn't have a pet creeper, I had to think of something else to ask for. I know what he really wanted to give me, a day on the throne leading the jungle. I can't think of a worse present for my birthday. I'd have to sit around all day while people come to see me and complain about what the other ocelots are doing. I've sat with dad in the throne room before and it was hard to stay awake. It was so dull!

But I could see how much it meant to dad to have me interested in his work, so I told him that I'd like to spend the day with him. I don't think I've ever seen him smile as much as he did when he heard me say that. I could count all his sharp, pointy teeth. He has a lot of them.

Now that I've thought a little more about it, I should have asked for a big pile of fish. At least they'd taste good. Instead, I've got to spend my birthday hanging around with dad when I could be out in the jungle having fun.

Oh well. I suppose it's just for one day. I can put up with being bored for just one day.

Day 2

One of the best things about being a royal kitten is that you can go wherever you like and nobody can tell you to go away. So today I went to the local village and read one of my favorite books of all time.

Diary of a Minecraft Creeper.

Creepers must exist if they can write a diary! I've read the book so many times that the cover is almost falling off. I should have asked dad to get me my own copy for my birthday, but he would only have told me not to be so stupid and forget all about creepers, but how can I forget about them when they sound so cool?

One of the most interesting parts of the book is when the creeper talks about being scared of ocelots. Why would they be scared of us? We're just cute, fluffy cats. And we really are very cute. I've seen my reflection in the lake. I have big, big eyes and a fuzzy little face, and if that wasn't enough to tell you that I look adorable, the fact that every Minecraftian I've ever met has always said "oh wow! Aren't you cute!" is a bit of a giveaway.

It makes me even more determined to meet a creeper. If they could only see that ocelots are lovely, then they wouldn't be afraid of us and then we could be best friends! I'd show them all my favorite places to hang out. We could go fishing together. I don't know if creepers eat fish but I bet that the creeper would love them if they just tasted it.

Day 3

It's my birthday tomorrow. I think dad is more excited about it than I am. I guess he's really excited about handing over the crown to me. I don't blame him. I think I'd be excited if there was someone else who could do his boring job.

That's it! Dad is trying to get out of being king because he's bored with listening to Minecraftians complain. Great. Nice birthday present – a life of boredom. You'd think he'd let me enjoy being a kitten for just a little bit longer.

Him and mom have been doing lots of whispering and pretending to hide things, like it's some big secret that I'm going to take over the throne in the morning. The only thing that could make my birthday special would be if they'd managed to smuggle in a creeper and they were going to wrap it up.

Could you imagine? Open up my presents and BOOM! A creeper explodes! It would be AWESOME!

Think of all the practical jokes you could play if you had a pet creeper. The look on dad's face when it explodes underneath his throne would be so funny! I'm pretty certain that creepers can put themselves back together again after they explode so I'd hide my creeper in all sorts of strange places to get dad when he's least expecting it. He'd never know what hit him!

If creepers don't put themselves together then who does? I mean, they don't just blow up and then die, do they? That would be really dumb.

If I get a pet creeper, I'd better find out how to put them back together when they explode before I play any tricks on dad. It would be really bad if I'd finally managed to get a pet creeper only to lose them over some stupid joke.

Day 4

Today was my birthday. It didn't go quite how I expected.

Mom did her best to make sure that I had a good time. She knew how much I wanted a pet creeper, so she got me a pet wolf. I can see why she thought it would be a good idea. Most people think that wolves are pretty cool. You can teach them tricks and stuff.

Thing is, I didn't want just any old pet. I wanted a creeper and no matter how cool wolves are, they're not a creeper. Now I've got this big, furry lump to look after.

I hope he doesn't want any of my fish. I don't mind sharing my fish with creepers, but I don't want to give my food to a wolf I didn't even want.

Still, I could tell that mom was really excited about the wolf and she really wanted to make me happy, so I smiled and pretended that I liked him. I named him Spot because he doesn't have any spots on him at all.

Then dad came and 'surprised' me with a day ruling the jungle. He was so proud of me. He kept introducing me to everyone. "This is my son, Slinklebert. He's going to be king one day."

I tried not to roll my eyes and pull faces behind his back, but it was so hard. OK, dad, we get it! I'm going to be king. That doesn't mean that I should have to spend my birthday hanging out in the throne room.

The first person to come into the throne room was an ocelot who was complaining that her sister had been tamed by a Minecraftian and was leaving the jungle. She wanted me to stop her from going.

I told her that she couldn't hold her sister back, but if she wanted to go with her, she was free to leave. Normally, ocelots aren't allowed to leave the jungle. If they do, they can never come back. But I told this one that she could return at any time. After all, eventually her sister is going to realize that Minecraftians are really boring and want to come home, so I figured that I could be generous and let them both explore the world for a bit.

I could tell that dad wasn't happy with my decision. He thinks that rules are rules and you shouldn't break them no matter what, but he put me in charge, so he had to go along with what I said otherwise he'd look stupid.

That gave me an idea. I decided to do the exact opposite of what I knew dad would want me to do. Maybe then I wouldn't have to sit around in the throne room all day again. So when two ocelots came along because they were having an argument over who got to eat a fish they caught, I ate the fish instead of sharing it between the two of them.

It was delicious.

I had so much fun. Dad got angrier and angrier, but there was nothing he could do. He'd said that I was king for a day and he couldn't change that.

At the end of the day, I made the most important decision of all. I gave myself permission to leave the jungle and come back.

When I announced my decree, there was uproar. "You can't leave the jungle!" cried dad. "I won't allow it."

"You don't have any choice," I reminded him. "I'm king for today and I've decided that I'm going to leave the jungle and look for a creeper. I'm going to prove once and for all that they really do exist."

"Slinklebert Petrovius Mordechai Smythe, you listen to me. I am your father and I say that you cannot go off on a wild goose chase like that. We need you here. What would your mom say if she knew that I'd let you leave the jungle to hunt for a creature that doesn't exist?"

"She'd say that sometimes a kitten needs to find these things out for themselves." Both of us jumped when mom spoke. We didn't realize that she'd come into the throne room. "Rodrick, if you didn't want Slinky to be king, then you shouldn't have put that crown on his head. As it is, as you well know, ocelot law means that Slinky can say whatever he likes and we have to obey him. If he wants to leave the jungle and look for creepers, then we have to let him go. I think this could be just what Slinky needs to grow up a little." She looked straight at me. "Perhaps seeing a bit of the world will show him that being king of the ocelots isn't such a bad thing after all."

"Do you mean it, mom?" I couldn't believe what I was hearing. I have the best mom in the world!

"Just make sure you take Spot with you, OK? That way, you can look after each other. I'm going to worry about you while you're gone and if Spot's with you, then at least I know that you have someone taking care of you."

"I will," I promised. I didn't really want that dumb old wolf following me around, but if it meant that mom would let me leave the jungle, then I'd put up with it.

Now I'm going to find a creeper and bring it back so everyone could see that they really do exist!

Day 5

"Now remember, keep Spot with you at all times and don't let him out of your sight. You can come home at any time, so if you get frightened on your first night away, just come back. Nobody will think anything bad of you for doing that. Have you got everything you need? Food?"

"Yes, mom," I sighed through the big grin on my face. I hadn't been able to stop smiling ever since mom and dad had agreed that I could leave the jungle. There was so much I wanted to see, I didn't know where to start. According to the creeper diary, you could find creepers all over Minecraftia, which makes it surprising that no ocelot has ever seen one, but maybe creepers are just really good at hiding. Maybe there is a whole colony of them living in the jungle, but they hide so well that they've remained undetected all this time.

Wouldn't that be funny?

"Come on, Mildred. Stop fussing over the boy. Can't you see that he wants to leave?" Dad's voice was gruff and I couldn't be sure, but I thought I saw a tear in the corner of his eye. Weird.

"I know, but Slinky's my baby. Can't a mother make a fuss about her baby on the day he leaves home?" mom sniffed.

"I'm coming back, you know."

"You jolly well better," said dad sternly. "Otherwise you're going to be in serious trouble!"

I gave mom and dad one last hug, checking that I had everything in my backpack, including some special cookies that mom had baked for me. Then I waved goodbye and set off down the path that led out of the jungle, Spot padding along by my side.

Freedom! What adventures we were going to have together. An ocelot and his wolf.

Day 6

The path that leads out of the jungle goes on FOREVER! Spot and I were walking for hours and hours, and we were still nowhere near the end of the jungle.

There was a part of me that thought that maybe it was a bad idea leaving home. It was very strange sleeping out under a tree instead of in my nice comfortable den, but the thought of finding creepers kept me going.

Spot is a real pain. He keeps jumping around and licking me on the face. Yuck! Then when I try to play catch the sunshine, he runs right in front of me so I can't jump properly.

He's a big, fat nuisance. I wish I'd left him at home. If mom thinks that wolves are such a good idea, then she should be the one to look after him.

Day 7

At last we reached the edge of the jungle.

Wow.

Spot and I stood at the edge of the trees, looking out over plains that seemed to go on forever. Most of it was covered in grass, but there were a few trees dotted here and there. I think this is what's called the savannah. It's nothing like anything I've ever seen.

In the distance, I could see some large four legged creatures running around. I'm really glad that I spent so much time reading in the library otherwise I might have been afraid of horses!

"Come on, Spot. Let's go!" Spot and I raced into the savannah. It felt so good to be able to run as fast as I could without worrying about running around trees. I could feel the wind rushing through my fur and I closed my eyes to enjoy the sensation.

Bad idea.

BANG! Just because there weren't as many trees in the savannah as the jungle didn't mean that there weren't *any* and I'd run straight into a large acacia tree.

Ouch, ouch and double ouch.

Spot whined and whimpered, pacing around me and licking my face as he tried to see if I was all right.

"Get off me, Spot!" I cried, pushing him away. My head hurt enough without adding wolf drool.

Lesson learned. No matter how excited I was, I'd pay more attention to where I was going in future. The last thing I wanted to do was run past any creepers without seeing them. How stupid would that be?

Day 8

Spot and I came across our first village today. An actual village with actual villagers!

At first, we stood at the outskirts of the village. I felt a bit shy about going in. This would be the first time I'd dealt with Minecraftians outside the jungle, and I didn't know how they would react to me. In the jungle, everyone knows that I'm a prince, destined to be king one day. Out here, am I just another ocelot?

An iron golem came pounding along the road. He stopped and stared at me.

I gulped. Iron golems are *really* big! I mean, they're enormous!

I didn't want him to see that I was afraid, so I stared right back at him.

Spot growled a little. "Be quiet, Spot!" I didn't want the iron golem to think that we were any kind of threat to the village. I didn't think that either of us would survive a battle with one, especially since there were other iron golems patrolling.

Suddenly, the iron golem reached forward. I closed my eyes, bracing myself for a powerful punch.

He didn't hit me.

I opened my eyes and saw that the iron golem was offering me a flower! How sweet of him.

I took it between my teeth and the iron golem stepped aside to let me go into the village. When he couldn't see me anymore, I put the flower in my backpack. I can't think what I can do with a flower, but it was a lovely gift and I'm going to treasure it.

"Hey! Ocelot! Do you want some fish?"

I looked over to see a villager in a brown robe standing by the roadside. He waved a piece of raw fish at me. It smelled really good, but I'd heard stories about what happened to ocelots who took fish from Minecraftians. They lose all their beautiful fur and become… a cat! A normal, boring, everyday kind of cat.

I might complain about being a prince, but I'd still rather be a royal ocelot than a common cat.

I hurried away from the Minecraftian and into the heart of the village.

There were lots of shops and stalls. Minecraftians and villagers mingled and traded, the air buzzing with the sound of their cries.

"Excuse me," I said to a passing villager. "Do you know where I can find any creepers?"

"Creepers?" The villager screamed. "Creepers are coming!"

"Aargh!" The rest of the villagers started screaming. "Creepers! Creepers!"

It was chaos, all the villagers and Minecraftians running around while the iron golems came out, looking everywhere for the creepers that they thought were coming into the village.

I decided to leave as quietly as I could before someone realized that it was a false alarm and blamed me for causing trouble.

Day 9

I still can't get over how different it is out of the jungle. Everything seems... I don't know how to describe it. More open. Less wild. If I'm honest, less exciting. In the jungle, there were so many trees to hide behind. You could play hide and pounce with the other ocelots, and not see your friends until they jumped out on you. In the savannah, there's no hiding place.

Spot and I tried to play a game anyway. Chase the tail is one of my favorites. You run round and round, trying to catch your own tail until you get worn out. Then you do it going the other way round.

Spot didn't understand the game. He thought that he was supposed to catch my tail! He nipped at it and it really hurt.

I wish mom had got me a creeper for a pet.

Speaking of which, there's still no sign of any creepers. In the jungle, everyone knows they're not real, but the villagers seemed to be really afraid of them. There must be some very scary stories about creepers. I can't imagine being so scared of something that's not real, so the way the villagers behaved makes me think that I'm right and the rest of the jungle animals are wrong – creepers are as real as the trees.

I still haven't seen any sign of one though. Are they trying to avoid me? Maybe creepers are just really, really good at hide and pounce. I haven't seen any signs of their tracks though, even though I've seen hoof prints from the horses and footprints from the Minecraftians.

If I could just get something with the scent of a creeper on it, I could get Spot to track them. Wolves are supposed to be really good at finding things using their sense of smell. I'd try anything to find a creeper. If Spot discovered some creepers for me, then maybe I'd think that he was a good pet after all.

Day 10

We came across a river today. It was wide and deep. Spot and I looked at each other and decided that we weren't going to try swimming across, at least, not at this point. It was a bit too far across.

Instead, we started to head upstream, looking for a better place to get to the other side. Watching the fish splashing about in the water made me hungry, so I decided to sit and have a snack. I opened up my backpack, but before I could get out any supplies, there was a splash as Spot jumped into the water!

A moment later, he was hauling himself back out, a fish in his mouth. He dropped it in front of me and sat there, wagging his tail in pleasure at how clever he was.

"All right, Spot. You can go and get another one."

The second I gave the word, Spot threw himself back into the water again.

"Clever dog you've got there." I looked round and saw a Minecraftian admiring Spot.

"He's not a dog, he's a wolf," I replied loftily.

"My mistake." The Minecraftian opened up his bag and took out a piece of fish. "It's a real shame, though. I was hoping to share some of my delicious fish with you."

I sniffed. His fish did smell good, but mom had always warned me about taking fish from strangers, so ignored it.

"Not interested?" The Minecraftian shrugged. "Oh well. I hope you don't mind if I make a fire here to cook some for myself. It's been a while since I've had anything to eat."

"Go ahead and do whatever you like. It's not my river."

"It might not be your river, but it's kind of you to let me camp with you anyway." The Minecraftian started gathering together some wood and soon he had a fire going. "My name is Matt."

I edged towards the fire. Now that it was getting dark, it was also getting cold and the warmth against my fur was comforting. "My name is Slinky," I told him.

"Nice to meet you, Slinky." Matt held out a hand and eventually I reached out with a paw and shook it. "I must say that I'm glad to see you here. I won't have to worry about creepers tonight thanks to you."

"What do you mean?"

"You don't know?" Matt shook his head. "How can you not know?"

"Not know what?"

"Creepers are terrified of ocelots!"

"No!" I couldn't believe it.

"It's true. Creepers are fearsome, terrifying creatures, but they're afraid of you little kitty cats. I can't think why. Look at you. You wouldn't hurt a fly."

I narrowed my eyes and flattened my ears. I knew an insult when I heard one and this Minecraftian was a little too smug for my liking. If he wasn't careful, he'd discover exactly what happened when you upset ocelot royalty. It wasn't pretty.

Matt laughed. "All right, Slinky. I can see that you're annoyed with me and I'm sorry. But I've never seen an ocelot before, and it's hard to imagine why creepers are so afraid of you. You're just so small!"

"That's because I'm still a kitten," I sniffed. He didn't need to know that I was smaller than all the other kittens my age. "That doesn't mean that I don't know how to take care of myself though."

"I don't doubt that for a second. After all, you're out in the plains all by yourself, heading towards the swamplands where some of the most fearsome monsters in Minecraftia live. You wouldn't be doing that if you didn't know how to take care of yourself. Well, either that or you're just the most stupid creature in Minecraftia."

I hissed.

"And you don't look stupid at all to me," Matt hastened to add.

"So tell me more about the creepers," I said. "Have you ever seen one?"

"Oh yes."

Matt had seen a creeper! They really were real!

Unless Matt was lying to me…

I decided to test him. "Creepers are purple, right?"

"No, they're green. Who told you they were purple?"

"Oh, no one," I shrugged. "But they do have eight legs, don't they?"

"No, just four. And a tall, long, thin body. You really don't know much about creepers, do you?"

"I'll have you know that I've read all the books about creepers in the jungle library. I've read *Diary of a Minecraft Creeper* five times."

"Have you now? So it's a good book, then?"

"Oh yes. It's my favorite. So full of action and adventure! It was *Diary of a Minecraft Creeper* that first gave me the idea of getting one as a pet."

"A creeper? As a pet?" Matt burst into laughter. "I've never heard anything so ridiculous."

"Hey! It's *not* ridiculous!" I was starting to really dislike Matt.

"Nobody can keep creepers as pets. If you try and put them in a cage, they'll just blow it up and take you with it. If you try and put them on a leash, they'll just blow themselves up and take you with them. If you try to tame them, they'll just blow themselves up and take you with them. Are you seeing a theme here?"

I had to admit that I was.

"But still," I persisted, "has anyone ever tried taming a creeper? I've heard a lot of stories about them, but nobody seems to have really taken the time to work with them."

"That's because they explode all the time!"

"Well maybe if you weren't all so mean to them, they wouldn't. Those poor creepers." I was more determined than ever to find one and take it home.

"Don't feel sorry for them," warned Matt. "Creepers are one of the most destructive creatures in Minecraftia. If I were you, I would stay as far away from them as possible."

I didn't like Matt and I had no intention of following his advice. The sooner I could find some creepers, the better.

Day 11

I am very glad that I brought Spot with me. I was right not to like Matt. He tried to steal all my things in the middle of the night!

I was woken up by Spot howling and growling. Matt had his hand on my bag, but Spot had it caught tight in his teeth and he wasn't going to let it go.

I was wide awake in an instant, my claws fully extended as I flew at Matt, scratching at his eyes.

He howled and put his hands up to defend himself against my attack. Spot took the opportunity to bite at his legs and Matt had no choice but to run away as fast as he could, leaving all his things behind.

The thief who'd tried to steal from me ended up losing all his things instead! That's what I call justice.

He had lots of things in his bag, most of which wasn't very interesting. I don't need a diamond pickaxe, and I can't imagine what I would do with a bunch of planks. However, he did have plenty of tasty fish and a few books that I hadn't read. It's always good to get new books to read. One of them seemed to be very special. The cover said 'enchanted book' and when I opened it up, it looked like it was full of magic spells! I don't know if I'd ever be able to cast any, but it was still very exciting to have an actual enchanted book of my very own.

Hopefully that's the last we'll see of Matt. I hate fighting with Minecraftians. In the jungle, they're only ever really nice to us, but I guess that's because they know we're royalty.

I wonder what Matt would have done if he knew that I was a prince?

Day 12

Spot and I found a place to cross the river where it wasn't too wide. It felt good to be on the other side. The further away from Matt we are, the better.

He was right about one thing though. We're now in swampland and I don't like it. Not one little bit. The ground is all soggy and damp. I hate getting my paws wet.

The sooner we get out of the swamp, the better. I can't imagine any creepers wanting to be somewhere as nasty as this.

Day 13

"Here, kitty, kitty, kitty! I've got some lovely fish for you! Don't you want to come and live with me?"

I ignored her. That was the third witch I'd seen who wanted me to move in with her. I don't understand why witches have such a fascination with ocelots.

One of them told me that a cat would help her spells be better. I don't know why. I've never cast a spell in my life. I've tried to read through the enchanted book I got from Matt, but it doesn't make any sense to me. It's full of strange symbols and pictures, and I've never heard of half of the things listed in there. Where am I supposed to get fermented spider eyes from? And how am I supposed to mix them all together? With my tail??

Spot doesn't like the swamp either. It's funny watching him trying to walk through. He puts his paw down on the ground and then lifts it up straight away, shaking off the water before putting it straight back down in the same place!

Hopefully we'll be out of the swamp soon. I'm not surprised that we haven't seen any creepers here. I wouldn't want to live in the swamp either.

Day 14

I saw a creeper! I saw a creeper!

At least, I *think* I saw a creeper. I'm almost positive that I did. Perhaps it was a very small zombie.

No, the more I think I about it, the more I'm certain that it was definitely a creeper. It's just so hard to be sure. It ran away before I could get a good look.

Spot and I were making our way through the swamp after seeing yet another witch. This must be Witch City or something. There are a lot of witch huts and when I found one without a witch in sight, I decided to go into it, just to see what it was like. After all, I've had so many witches wanting me to move in with them, I figured that I should see what their home is like, just in case I decided to give up being a royal kitten and become a witch's cat instead.

There's no way I'm going to be a witch's cat. Have you seen the inside of a witch's hut? It's TINY! And it smells really funny as well. Maybe it's all the potion ingredients that they keep, but it was like going into a large garbage heap with a side order of cow dung. Spot wouldn't even put his nose inside the room, it smelled so bad. He ran off into the swamp, yelping.

I stayed around a bit longer, hoping to find something interesting. There was a chest, but it only had a couple of potion bottles in it. There wasn't even any fish! I don't see how a witch thinks that she could look after me if they don't have plenty of fish in their cupboard.

It didn't take long to see everything there was to see. Just when I turned to leave, I saw it. The creeper!

It was standing at the edge of the clearing. It was hard to see because it was almost the same color as the trees and bushes around it, which is why it's possible that it was a zombie. Dad always told me to keep an open mind about things until you're absolutely sure.

But zombies groan and this thing hissed a bit before running off into the undergrowth. I tried to chase after it, but my nose wasn't working as well as it usually does because it was still full of the scent of witch hut and I soon lost sight of it.

I called for Spot and he came bounding out of the trees. He was happy that I was out of the hut, but when I asked him to find the creeper, he just looked at me, head to one side, as if to say *are you mad?*

Whatever it was, I'm going to find it tomorrow and then I'll know for certain if it was a creeper.

Day 15

Spot and I spent all day wandering around the swamp and we didn't see anything except more witches.

"Are you sure you don't want this lovely fish?" called one from her hut. I looked over and saw that she was waving some cooked fish at me. Everyone knows that cooked fish tastes disgusting. I don't know why she thought that I would like it.

"Have you seen any creepers?" I asked her.

"Lots," came the reply.

"Can you tell me where they are?"

"Oh, you wanted to know if I'd seen any creepers *today*." A look of cunning came over the witch's face. "Well, I haven't seen any this morning, but if you agreed to live with me, I'm sure that I could help you find one. There are plenty of them in the swamp."

Something told me that the witch would never find a creeper for me and I'd just be stuck in her strange smelling hut, brewing potions all day long.

"Thanks, but I think we'll just find one for ourselves."

The witch pouted and stamped her foot, and I knew that I'd made the right choice.

Still, it's getting harder and harder to know what to do. I've been away from home for over a week now and I'm not any closer to getting a pet creeper.

"What do you think, Spot? Shall we leave the swamp and go somewhere else?"

The howl of joy Spot let out startled the birds from the trees and the pigs from the bushes. Spot spent the next few minutes chasing them around, trying to catch his supper.

Maybe once we're away from this miserable place, we'll have a lot more luck. After all, if Spot and I hate getting our feet wet, creepers probably do too. We're going to head for the hills. That should give us a really good view of the land around and we can try to see some creepers from there.

Day 16

At last, Spot and I are free of the swamp. There were more plains on the other side, and it felt so good to be able to run without getting our paws wet or worrying about bumping into witches with their rotten, cooked fish.

As we raced along, Spot nipped at me and I ran at him, trying to knock him over (of course, I couldn't) which became one of the best games of tag I've ever played. I forgot all about creepers, witches, swamps, and cooked fish and just had fun.

It's what being a kitten is all about.

When we'd had enough, we flopped down under the shade of a tree, all worn out from playing.

And that was when I saw it. The creeper!

It was definitely a creeper and not a zombie or a bush or a strange shaped tree. It looked just like the picture on the cover of *Diary of a Minecraft Creeper*, all tall and thin and green. I even heard a strange hissing sound coming from its direction.

"Spot! Look over there! Can you see what I can see?"

I nudged Spot, who sat up and turned to see what I was pointing at, but the creeper was startled by the movement and disappeared off again.

Spot shook his head and settled back down, resting his head on his paws, but I couldn't relax now that I knew that creepers were real. I must be the first ocelot in the history of Minecraftia to see a creeper!

Pressing myself close to the ground so that I was hard to see, I snuck over to where the creeper had been. The grass was a little flatter where it had been standing, and I could see a few broken twigs on the bush that it had run behind, but its trail soon disappeared.

"Come on, Spot. Help me find the creeper."

Spot came over and put his nose to the ground, trying to pick up the scent of the creeper, but after a while he looked at me and did a wolf's best impression of a shrug.

He had no idea where it had gone.

I wonder if it was the same one that I'd seen in the swamp the other day? Was it following me? Maybe it wants to be friends with me, but is feeling shy?

I'm going to have to figure out a way to get the creeper to talk to me. I just know we're going to be best friends!

Day 17

Spot and I have set up camp on the plains. We've found a nice tree for shelter, and Spot curls up at the base while I climb up and stretch out along one of the branches. Now that we've found a creeper, I'm going to do my best to make friends with it.

What would a creeper like as a present? I'm not quite sure. The diary I read didn't really talk much about what creepers would like.

Mom is always happy when I bring her flowers. Maybe the creeper would like some flowers as well.

There were lots of large, yellow flowers growing around, so I started picking them. Spot tried to help me, but it's really difficult to pick flowers when you're a wolf. He'd try to bite them off, but all that would happen was that he'd get lots of drool over the flowers and then he'd pull them out of the ground, completely destroying the flower.

It's much easier to pick flowers when you're an ocelot. I just put out a claw and with one quick swipe, I had a flower.

After a while, Spot got bored with picking flowers and he ran off to chase some horses, but I kept working until I had a huge bunch of flowers.

I put most of them in a big pile, and then put some flowers on the ground in a trail leading to the pile. Once I thought the trail was long enough, I raced back to the pile of flowers and hid behind a bush to wait for the creeper to arrive.

I waited a long time. It got very boring. I was tempted to go and join Spot with the horses, but I kept thinking of the creeper I'd seen and I decided to wait for a bit longer. If the creeper didn't show up by tonight, then I'd just have to think of something else to try.

The sun had just started to set when I saw him. At least, I think it's a him. It's hard to tell with creepers.

He was walking slowly along the trail of flowers I'd left, sniffing at each one before moving on to the next. When it reached the big pile of flowers, it stared at it for a while before diving headfirst into it! All I could see was a set of creeper legs waving around in the air!

I couldn't help laughing. Unfortunately, when the creeper heard me, it got up and raced away, but that's OK. I'll get some more flowers tomorrow for him and maybe he'll stay longer next time.

Day 18

I spent all day gathering flowers again. This time, I got Spot to bury me in the pile of flowers so that the creeper wouldn't know that I was there.

It's very uncomfortable hiding among flowers. The petals kept tickling my nose, and it was very hard not to sneeze. And it was even more boring than waiting behind the bush. At least when I was over there, I could watch Spot playing. I can't see anything inside the pile of flowers.

Luckily, ocelots have a very good sense of hearing, so I could hear the creeper coming close. Once again, it took its time, sniffing at each of the flowers as it moved along the trail I'd left for it.

I lay there, still as a statue, hardly daring to breathe in case it scared the creeper. Suddenly, it thrust its head into the middle of the flowers and there I was. Face to face with a creeper. An actual creeper, so close that all I had to do was reach out a paw and I could touch it!

HISS!

The creeper let out a loud noise and jumped back. I leaped out of the flowers after it. "Don't go!" I cried. "I just want to be your friend!"

I don't think creepers speak the same language as ocelots. It started running away.

"Please don't go," I begged.

The creeper stopped and looked over its shoulder at me.

"Please?"

For a moment, I thought the creeper was going to come back. It certainly seemed to be considering it. But then it turned around and carried on running, disappearing off into the distance.

I shall try again tomorrow. I'm definitely getting closer to winning its trust.

Day 19

As I gathered more sunflowers for the creeper, I hummed a little tune to myself.

Creeper mine, creeper mine,

With eyes so black and skin so fine,

Creeper green, creeper green,

I know you're real! You have been seen!

Once more, I built up a pile of sunflowers for the creeper while Spot went off to play with the horses. I think he's happier here than he ever was in the jungle. There's so much space for him to run around. He's been having races with the horses. I'm sure they let him win – those horses are fast!

I got so distracted watching Spot run around with the horses that I didn't realize that the creeper was coming. It wasn't until I heard some rustling in the pile that I saw him there, burying himself in the flowers again.

"Hello," I said quietly.

The creeper froze.

"Don't be afraid. I'm not going to hurt you."

The creeper stayed completely still, its legs sticking out of the pile.

"You do look funny like that, you know."

The legs wriggled a bit, but the creeper stayed where he was.

"My name is Slinky," I told it. "What's yours?"

Silence.

"I'm from the jungle. Nobody believes in creepers there. We've never seen one. I think I'm the first ocelot to meet a creeper. I'd love it if you came home with me so I could show you to my parents."

The creeper jumped back from the pile, a terrified look on its face.

"What's wrong?"

The creeper started shivering.

"You aren't afraid of ocelots... are you?"

The creeper shook even harder.

"You don't need to be scared of me. I'm not going to hurt you and I won't let any of the other ocelots hurt you either. I'm going to be king of the jungle one day, you know. If I say that nobody is allowed to hurt you, then nobody will hurt you. You're safe with me."

The creeper started shaking harder, backing away. Its mouth opened and shut as if it were trying to say something, but I couldn't make out the words.

"What's that? Is there something wrong?" I edge towards the creeper not wanting to frighten it away, but before I had the chance to figure out what it was saying my world went black.

"A royal kitten, you say? You're even more valuable than I thought."

I recognized that voice. It was Matt. He'd captured me!

Day 20

I can't believe that I let myself be caught by Matt. I *knew* I couldn't trust him.

Matt put me in a cage and now I was on the back of a wagon being pulled along to goodness knows where.

"Do you know how long I've been waiting to find an ocelot kitten?" he said. "I'm going to be rich beyond my wildest dreams! There are a lot of people who've been after a cat just like you, and I'm going to let them outbid each other until I have all the diamonds I could ever want."

"Oh no. You're not going to sell me to a witch, are you?"

Matt laughed. "A witch? They can't afford you. No, I have much bigger plans than that for you, my friend."

"I'm not your friend."

Matt shrugged. "Suit yourself. It doesn't make any difference to me. I'm still going to sell you."

50

I looked through the bars of the cage trying to see Spot. Surely he'd come to rescue me?

There was no sign of him. So much for him protecting me. He was probably still off with the horses and hadn't even realized I'd been catnapped.

Matt pulled his horse to a halt. "Right. This looks like a good place to take shelter for the night. Normally I'd keep moving because of all the creepers in the area, but now that I've got you, I don't have to worry."

"What do you mean?"

"Didn't you know?" Matt shook his head. "You're even more stupid than you look. Creepers are afraid of ocelots. I have no idea why. Look at you. You're a scrawny little thing that wouldn't stand a chance in a fight. I could beat you with one hand tied behind my back."

"Why don't you let me out of the cage and we'll see if that's right?" I said slyly.

"Do I look as dumb as an ocelot?" Matt chuckled. "Nice try, but you're staying right in that cage until your new owner has paid for you. Then it's up to them whether they want to see how well you can fight. Something tells me that they'll have other plans in mind for you."

He started a fire and pulled out some fish from his bag. "Do you want some?"

I really did. I was starving. But I didn't want to take anything from Matt, so I shook my head.

"All right. Suit yourself. Don't complain if you're hungry later because all the food will be gone."

He started cooking the fish, the smell of the cooking meat turning my stomach. I don't understand why humans insist on spoiling their fish like that. They taste so much nicer raw.

Once he'd finished eating, Matt burped, wiped his hands down the front of his shirt and lay down to sleep next to the fire. "I suggest that you get some rest, cat," he told me. "I want you to look your best when you meet your potential owners."

It wasn't long before he was snoring, leaving me pacing up and down inside the cage wondering how I was going to break free and escape.

Day 21

I tried all night to break through the bars but it was impossible. I even broke a tooth trying to chew through them. Luckily it was just one of my baby teeth, but it still hurt.

I don't know what I'm going to do. Spot is nowhere to be seen, and Matt has been talking about how it's not long to go before we reach the market and then he's going to sell me.

Sell me! I'm a royal kitten, not a slave. He has no right to sell me.

He offered me some more fish for breakfast, but I turned my nose up at it. I'd rather starve than accept anything from Matt. Anyway, he's going to find it difficult to sell me if I'm all skinny and miserable looking.

Maybe I could disguise myself as a creeper!

I reached a paw out through the bars and tried to grab some leaves, but I couldn't get them to stick to my body. When Matt saw what I was trying to do, he burst out laughing.

"Nice try, kitten, but nobody is going to mistake you for a creeper. Now be a good cat and let me comb your fur."

He opened the door of the cage and reached out to brush me. I saw my opportunity and tried to push past him, claws extended, hissing, and spitting all the way.

To my surprise, Matt stepped out of my way. That was easy! Freedom at last!

Just as I was about to dart off into the bushes, I felt something land around my neck. Matt had thrown a lasso around me!

He yanked me back to his feet. "Now, now, cat. I told you. You're not going anywhere until I've sold you, so you might as well stop fighting and accept that this is what's going to happen. If you didn't want an owner, you shouldn't have left the jungle. Now sit still and let me make you look pretty."

Of course I didn't sit still. I was all arms and legs, wriggling and squirming and doing my best to make it impossible to groom me.

SPLASH!

All of a sudden, I was drenched! Matt had thrown a bucket
of water over me. "Let that be a lesson," he said sternly. "If
you keep this up, I'll forget about selling you and there'll
be lava in that bucket next time. I've told you. There's no
way you're going to escape me, so be a good kitten and you
won't get hurt."

I sat down and shut up, but inwardly I was seething. There
had to be a way to escape Matt, there just had to be.

Day 22

The biggest indignity of all. Matt put a bow around my neck today. He said it would make me look pretty so that people would pay more.

He also told me that if I didn't purr and behave nicely when the buyers were looking at me, he'd bring out his bucket again. I don't know what to do.

He said that we'll reach town tomorrow so if I haven't escaped by then, I'm doomed. I haven't eaten anything for days now and I'm starting to feel really weak. It was almost enough to persuade me to take some of the fish Matt offered me this morning, but I managed to be strong and say no.

I don't know if I'll be able to say no to my new owner though. My tummy is rumbling all the time. It's so loud that you can hear it over the fire. Matt says that if I don't eat something before we get to the market, he's going to force feed me.

I'll spit it back in his face. I don't care if he does pour a bucket of lava over me. Maybe that would be better than spending the rest of my life as someone's slave.

We camped at the foot of a hill. Matt says the village we're going to is just on the other side and we'll be there in the morning. There was a time when I would have been really excited about going to a village, but I just want to go home.

Day 23

Creepers are amazing! They're the most intelligent, beautiful creatures in the world ever. I'm so glad that I came out looking for them.

Matt was asleep by the campfire last night. I was wide awake. I was too hungry and nervous to sleep, so I was pacing my cage, trying to find a weakness that might let me out.

My tummy was rumbling so loudly that I almost didn't hear it at first, but as the creeper drew nearer, I heard a hissing sound and I looked over to see Spot and the creeper looking through the bars of the cage at me.

"Spot! Creeper!" I gasped. "What are you doing here?"

Matt snorted loudly and I looked over at him, frightened that he'd woken up.

"Have you come to rescue me?" I whispered.

The creeper bowed its head. It had! I was saved!

Spot and the creeper tried to open the door of the cage, but it was locked. "Matt has the key," I told them. "It's in his coat pocket."

Spot and the creeper looked over to where Matt was using his coat as a pillow. There was no way that they were going to be able to get the key without waking him up.

That didn't stop Spot from trying though.

He crept over to Matt and nudged his head gently with his nose. Matt laughed and rolled over in his sleep. "Stop it, Maria!" he giggled. "That tickles."

Spot froze while Matt got comfortable again and was soon snoring again.

My wolf tried a different approach, taking the coat between his teeth and gently tugging at it. Slowly but surely, he eased the coat out from under Matt's head. I couldn't believe it! Spot was going to get the keys!

Just as Spot tugged the last bit of the coat out, Matt's head bumped down, waking him up. He sat up, rubbing the sore spot where he'd been hit. "Well, well, well," he murmured. "What do we have here? I remember you. You're Slinky's pet wolf. Perfect! I know plenty of people who'll pay for a tame wolf as well. Looks like it's going to be a great day for me at the village market!"

He sat up, reaching around for a leash, and that's when he saw it. The creeper. It had crept up behind Matt without him knowing and it hissed as loudly as it could, right in Matt's face.

HISS!

"Aargh! Creeper!"

Matt jumped up and raced off in the direction of the village, leaving all his things behind. Once again, I had all his stuff!

Spot came back to the cage carrying the keys in his mouth. It took a while for him to fit the key in the lock, but eventually the cage door popped open and I was free.

"Spot! Creeper! You saved me!"

I gave Spot a big hug and reached out to the creeper to join us. For a moment, it just stood there, watching, but at last it came over and the three of us hugged and laughed as we thought about Matt and how scared he'd been when he saw creeper.

Day 24

All that time Spot spent running around with the horses was more than just fun and games. It turns out that he made a lot of friends with the horses, and he persuaded two of them to pull the carriage that had the cage.

The creeper and I sat in the cage with the door open while Spot ran ahead with the horses, showing them the way to go. This is the way to travel! We'll get back to the jungle in no time.

The creeper and I looked at each other. "Thank you for saving me," I said.

"You're welcome."

I started. "You speak Minecraftian!"

"Of coursssse. All creepersss do. We jussst don't bother mossst of the time. Mossst Minecraftiansss are really ssstupid. It'sss much more fun to blow them up."

I laughed. "I bet it is! But what made you decide to rescue me?"

"You're the firssst Minecraftian to give me flowersss," the creeper replied simply. "I like flowersss."

"I'm glad you liked them. I really wanted to make friends with you. I've always wanted to meet a creeper. My name's Slinky."

"My name'sss Colin."

"Pleased to meet you, Colin." I reached out a paw for him to shake and after a moment, Colin reached out a foot and took it.

"Did you know that the other ocelots don't believe that creepers exist?" I told him. "I can't wait to get back home and show you to everyone."

"Home? Ssshow me to everyone?" Colin turned a pale green. "You mean, take me to the jungle? Oh no. I couldn't possssibly."

My heart sank. ""Why not?"

"Well everyone knows that ocelotsss are evil. The moment they sssee a creeper, they tear them to ssshredsss. It's much worssse than exploding. At leasssst when we blow oursssselvesss up, we can put oursssselvesss together again afterwardsss. When an ocelot'sss finissshed with you, that'sss it. You're dead."

My jaw dropped. "Who told you that? It's not true and I should know. I'm going to be king of the ocelots one day."

"King of the ocelotsss?" Colin tried to bow, but there wasn't much room in the cage.

"Don't do that," I told him. "It's OK. You're a friend and friends don't bow down to each other."

"Friend?" Colin said the word as if it were new to him. "I've never had a friend who wasssn't a creeper."

"Well, you do now."

Colin smiled at me and I smiled back. I didn't want a creeper for a pet anymore. It was much better to have them as friends.

Day 25

Traveling in a horse drawn carriage is so much faster than running, and it's more comfortable too. As we rode, Colin told me more about life as a creeper. It's fascinating. I've learned so much more from him than I ever did from a book.

Creepers are really rather social creatures, but they're also very shy. I suppose I would be shy too if every time I saw someone they ran away screaming or tried to kill me. It's a shame because they just want to be friends, but after years of being hunted, they've decided to try and avoid Minecraftians – or blow them up.

Colin says that every year the creepers hold a competition to see who can blow up the most Minecraftians. His dad holds the creeper record for most explosions in one night, and Colin told me that he wants to beat his record one day and make his dad proud of him.

I told Colin all about being a royal kitten. He said that he'd love it if he got to tell people what to do all day, but when I explained how boring it is in the throne room, Colin decided that he'd prefer being a creeper after all.

They have a game called Boom Tag. It's like kitten tag only when you catch someone, they have to try and blow you up. It sounds like fun, but not the kind of game a kitten can play. We're not as good at putting ourselves together again after an explosion...

Day 26

It turns out that there's a much easier way to get round to the jungle. We didn't need to go through the swamp at all. Colin gave us directions along the river and it was so much nicer. The horses didn't have to struggle through the boggy ground and I didn't have to hold my nose against the smell.

The way we were going we were going to be home in no time and I stretched out in the cage, soaking up the sunshine while Colin sat next to me, looking at the surroundings.

Suddenly, the horses lurched to a halt, jolting Colin and me forward.

I leaped to my feet, turning to see what had stopped us.

Creepers! A whole group of them blocking our path. I had no idea that there were so many.

"You have ssstolen one of our own!" hissed their leader. "Give him back!"

"Give him back! Give him back!" The creepers started chanting, making an alarming noise.

"They're getting ready to explode," whispered Colin. "I need to go and calm them down."

He jumped out of the cage and ran round to talk to the creepers.

"Colin!" A creeper rushed forward and hugged him. "I wasss ssso worried about you."

"I'm fine, mom. I was jussst helping my friend, Ssslinky. He got captured and I freed him."

"But you were in a cage! They were taking you away!"

"The cage wasssn't locked," Colin explained. "We jussst thought that it would be a niccce way to travel. I've never been in a horssse drawn carriage before. It'sss fun!"

I jumped out, going to stand next to Colin so I could tell his family how brave he'd been.

"An occcelot!" screamed the creepers. "Run!"

"No! Wait!" Colin and I shouted together, waving our arms to get their attention.

The creepers stopped rushing around, standing so still you'd think that they were frozen.

"Ssslinky isssn't like other occcelots," Colin explained. "He'sss my friend. And he'sss not jussst my friend. He'sss going to be king of the jungle one day."

"King?" The creepers started talking to each other and slowly, one by one, they knelt down before me, bowing to the ground.

"Please. Don't do that. There's no need. Colin saved me. It's me that should bow down to you."

I knelt down on the ground and bowed to the creepers. They gasped when they saw what I was doing.

"My friends, I have a favor to ask you. I'd like you to let Colin come back with me to the jungle so I can show the other ocelots that creepers are real and they are friendly. I promise you that when I become king, I will pass a law that means that an ocelot will never be allowed to attack a creeper. You have nothing to be scared of!"

The creepers looked at each other and I could hear muttering as they discussed whether Colin should be allowed to come with me.

"All right," said his mom. "Colin can go with you. But if anything happens to him, I will bring all the creepers with me and we will explode in the middle of the jungle. I don't care how frightened we are of ocelots."

I looked into her eyes and I could see how serious she was. "Don't worry," I assured her. "Colin will be safe with me.

Day 27

At last, we were at the outskirts of the jungle. I jumped out of the cage and went round to see the horses. "Thank you for taking us all this way. I think you should go back to the plains now. We can walk from here."

The horses whinnied, but stood where they were.

"What is it? What's wrong?"

Spot came and sat in front of me. He howled and then looked back at the horses before howling at me again.

"You want to go with the horses? Is that it?"

Spot nodded.

I sniffed. "I'm going to miss you, Spot. I couldn't have found Colin without you. You've been the best pet wolf an ocelot could want. Are you sure you want to leave?"

Spot nodded again.

"All right, my friend. Run free with the horses. But you can come back to the jungle any time you like. You're always welcome."

Spot darted forward and licked my face before running back with the horses towards the plains.

I watched him go, trying not to cry.

"You did the right thing." Colin came and stood next to me as Spot disappeared into the distance. "I know how much Ssspot meant to you."

"I just want him to be happy," I shrugged. "The stupid thing is that I didn't want a pet wolf but now that he's gone, I realize that he was the best birthday present I've ever had."

"I'm sssure he'll come back," Colin said. "He'll always be your friend."

"I hope so."

Colin and I watched until we couldn't see Spot anymore and then we turned and headed into the jungle.

Day 28

It felt good to be home. I'd enjoyed exploring Minecraftia and discovering all the strange, exotic creatures out there, but there was nothing like the smells and sounds of the jungle.

Now that I was back, I didn't think I'd ever leave again.

"OK, Colin," I said. "Tomorrow we'll reach the throne room and I can show you to all my family. They're going to be so surprised when they see that creepers really do exist." A thought struck me. "I know! Why don't we play a trick on them?"

A slow smile spread across Colin's face as he listened to my idea. "That sssoundsss like fun," he grinned as we headed off to find the things we'd need.

Tomorrow, my parents were going to get the biggest shock of their lives!

Day 29

A very strange creature walked into the throne room by my side today.

"Slinky!"

"Slinky's home!"

"Good to see you, Slinky!"

At first, everyone was so excited to see me that they didn't notice the being by my side. Mom and dad came rushing up to hug me and I was surrounded by ocelots and other jungle creatures all wanting to pat me on the back and welcome me home.

Colin coughed and it was then that my parents noticed him. "Who's this that you've brought with you, Slinky?"

"This is my good friend, Colin. He's a-" I paused and grinned. "Well, I'll let you guess what he is."

I could tell that Colin was getting nervous, and I smiled at him reassuringly to let him know that it was OK – nobody was going to hurt him.

Dad walked over to him, looking him up and down. "Most peculiar," he said at last. "He looks a little like a pig, only he's tall instead of long."

"And he's such a strange color," Mom added. I grinned. We'd covered Colin with flower petals earlier to disguise his green skin, but it still shone through the petals, giving him an eerie glow.

"I'm sorry. This is terribly rude of me. What's your name?" dad asked.

"Colin."

"Colin. Nice to meet you. I'm King Rodrick." Dad reached out a paw and after a moment's hesitation, Colin took it. I stifled a giggle at the thought of the king of the jungle shaking hands with a creeper and he didn't even know it.

"Where are you from, Colin?" mom asked.

"The Sunflower Plains," Colin replied. "Just past the swamp."

"Fascinating. I've never seen a sunflower before. What do they look like?" Mom walked right up to him. Even though I'd promised Colin that nobody would hurt him, he couldn't help but shake with fear. I guess it's hard to think of ocelots as your friends when you've spent your whole life being told that they're mean and evil.

Colin's shivering shook all the flower petals off, revealing his green skin. Everyone gasped.

"Is that-?"

"No! It's can't be!"

It started as a murmur that built up to a roar. "It's a creeper! It's really a creeper!"

I held up my paws for silence. "Yes, everyone. I'd like to introduce my best friend, Colin the creeper. It's thanks to Colin and Spot that I was able to come back home."

"What do you mean?" Mom looked anxious. "Slinky, where's Spot?"

"He's back on the plains. Don't worry, mom. Spot wanted to stay and I thought it was only fair, since it was him and Colin who saved me from Matt, an evil Minecraftian who wanted to sell me."

"Sell you??"

I sat down on the throne, my family and friends gathered around me, as I told them all about my adventures in Minecraftia looking for creepers. When I told them how Matt had caught me, mom screamed. "I *knew* I should never have let you go!"

"It's fine, mom," I laughed. "Look, I'm sitting right in front of you, aren't I? I got back home safely, and now that I've seen a little bit of the world, I know that there's nowhere I'd rather be than right here. Dad, I just wanted to tell you that I didn't want to be king before I left, but now that I've seen what it's like out in Minecraftia, there's nothing I'd rather be. I've built friendships with the creepers and if the ocelots ever need help again, they'll be there for us – just as we'll be there for them."

"Thank you, Colin, for looking after Slinky," said mom warmly. "You've been a true friend to him."

"You're welcome," said Colin. "Ssslinky'sss the firssst persson to give me flowersss. He'sss my bessst friend."

"You're my best friend, too, Colin," I told him. "You and Spot."

Day 30

Colin left to go home today, but he said he'd come back again for a visit really soon. He might even bring a couple of other creepers with him. This could be the start of the creeper exchange program!

I told Colin to say hi to Spot when he gets back to the plains. I wonder if I'll ever see Spot again? I have a funny feeling that mom is going to get me another pet wolf, but it won't be the same as Spot.

Maybe I can get Spot to bring some horses to the jungle. That would be amazing!

Dad has been really excited about handing the crown over to me. He told me a secret, he finds being king just as boring as I do! He said that he's been inspired by my adventures and he wants to go out and travel the world too. He's very curious about witches and what their huts look like. I told him they smell really bad, but I don't think he believed me. I guess it's hard to imagine anything that smells as bad as a witch's hut.

I think the real reason he wants to go exploring is to find Matt. I wish the creepers had blown him up. I hate the thought that Matt is out there somewhere, hunting for ocelot kittens to sell. If dad doesn't find him then, when I'm bigger I'm going to go looking for him and once I find him… well, he'd wish that he'd never tried to sell me.

In the meantime, I've got lots more work to do in the throne room. Dad is putting me in charge of sorting out arguments. Today I have to deal with a pair of ocelots who are having an argument about creepers and how big their explosions are.

I think I might have to get Colin to come back and do a demonstration.

When I went to my den, I found that Colin had left me a little present. A sunflower. I didn't see him bring it with him, but it's sitting by my bed as a reminder of the fun times we had.

A creeper is the best friend an ocelot could have. I just hope that one day I get the chance to repay him for everything he's done for me.

Made in the USA
Lexington, KY
20 December 2017